The Drunken City

by

Adam Bock

SAMUEL FRENCH

FOUNDED 1830

NEW YORK HOLLYWOOD LONDON TORONTO

SAMUELFRENCH.COM

ISBN 978-0-573-66288-1   Printed in U.S.A.   #6258

**IMPORTANT BILLING AND CREDIT
REQUIREMENTS**

All producers of *THE DRUNKEN CITY* must give credit to the Author of the Play in all programs distributed in connection with performances of the Play, and in all instances in which the title of the Play appears for the purposes of advertising, publicizing or otherwise exploiting the Play and/or a production. The name of the Author *must* appear on a separate line on which no other name appears, immediately following the title and *must* appear in size of type not less than fifty percent of the size of the title type.

Playwrights Horizons, Inc., New York City, produced the New York City Premiere of "THE DRUNKEN CITY" Off-Broadway in 2008

"THE DRUNKEN CITY" was commissioned by and originally premiered in July 2005 at Kitchen Theatre Company, Ithaca, NY Rachel Lampert, Artistic Director. The Play was subsequently revised during a developmental workshop with Theatre Works of Palo Alto, CA Robert Kelley, Artistic Director

PLAYWRIGHTS HORIZONS

Tim Sanford
Artistic Director

Leslie Marcus
Managing Director

William Russo
General Manager

presents

THE DRUNKEN CITY

A new play by
ADAM BOCK

Featuring

Cassie Beck   Mike Colter   Maria Dizzia
Barrett Foa   Sue Jean Kim   Alfredo Narciso

Scenic Design	Costume Design	Lighting Design	Sound Design
David Korins	Jenny Mannis	Matthew Richards	Bart Fasbend•

Original Music	Choreography	Casting by	Director of Developm•
Michael Friedman	John Carrafa	Alaine Alldaffer C.S.A.	Jill Garland

Production Manager	Press Representative	Production Stage Manager
Shannon Nicole Case	The Publicity Office	Bess Marie Glorioso

Directed by
TRIP CULLMAN

The Drunken City was commissioned by and originally premiered in July 2005 at Kitchen Theatre Company, Ithaca NY, Rachel Lampert, Artistic Director. The play was subsequently revised during a developmental workshop with TheatreWorks of Palo Alto, CA, Robert Kelley, Artistic Director

Playwrights Horizons gratefully acknowledges The Peter Jay Sharp Foundation for its very generous support of *The Drunken City*.

The Drunken City has received generous support from the Andrew W. Mellon Foundation, the Jerome Foundation, and the National Endowment for the Arts.

Special thanks to The Harold and Mimi Steinberg Charitable Trust for supporting new plays at Playwrights Horizons.

Special thanks to Time Warner Inc. for its leadership support of The American Voice: New Play and Musical Theater Development at Playwrights Horizons.

CAST

The Guys:
EDDIE
FRANK

The Bachelorette Party:
MARNIE
LINDA
MELISSA

Another Guy:
BOB

All in their mid to late twenties.

ONE.

(MARNIE, MELISSA and LINDA enter. They look around.)

MELISSA. Any way any way.

Ok Marnie? Ready Linda? Ok? Show them.

(All three show the audience their engagement rings.)

Isn't that weird? We're all engaged. All three of us.
It was kind of amazing because we all got them Well,
you know, Jack gave Linda her ring

MARNIE. Wait a sec Melissa.

MELISSA. What?

MARNIE. This is Jack.

(Takes out, unfolds a large xerox copy of a photo of Jack.)

LINDA. You brought a picture of Jack?

MARNIE. Yeah I figured it would be easier if they saw a
photo.

LINDA. That's such a good picture of him.

MARNIE. I know right?

MELISSA. Um

LINDA. When did you take it?

MARNIE. Remember the other day And I had it printed big
at Kinkos.

LINDA. Can I have it?

MARNIE. Sure.

MELISSA. Ok ok ok.

So Linda got hers from Jack and then Gary gave Marnie
her ring

MARNIE. Just a sec. This is Gary.

(MARNIE unfolds, shows large xerox photo of Gary.)

MELISSA. Did you bring pictures of everyone?

MARNIE. Stories are always way better with a visual aid.

LINDA. Did you bring one of me?

MELISSA. Why would she bring one of you? You're here.

LINDA. Oh

MARNIE. So I didn't. My ring's pretty isn't it. He picked it out himself! Hhht.

LINDA. When Jack asked me to marry him I got so nervous I went into my room and I took my bottle of Windex and I cleaned my sneakers.

MARNIE. You did?

MELISSA. I was upset because Jack asked Linda and then Gary and Marnie, so when I saw Linda's ring and then I saw Marnie's ring I was upset.

MARNIE. You were?

LINDA. You were?

MARNIE. Why were you upset?

MELISSA. You'd have been upset too if Linda and me'd come and shown you Look Look

LINDA. Did we sound like that?

MARNIE. We didn't sound like that

LINDA. We were like Look Look?

MELISSA. You were supposed to be happy You were happy

MARNIE. Were you mad at us?

MELISSA. No. No. No.

MARNIE. So why didn't you say something?

MELISSA. I didn't want to say anything because I was happy for you.

MARNIE. I didn't even know you were upset. Did you know she was upset?

LINDA. No.

MARNIE. Cause I didn't know she was upset.

MELISSA. I didn't want to say anything.

LINDA. Did you tell Kelly you were mad?

MELISSA. I wasn't mad.

LINDA. Did you tell Lori?

MELISSA. You both had rings. I didn't have a ring.

MARNIE. But that's

MELISSA. But then Jason he

MARNIE. Ok just a sec Wait wait This is Jason.

(Unfolds, shows large xerox photo of Jason.)

LINDA. How upset were you?

MARNIE. Yeah?

MELISSA. But then Jason

MARNIE. That makes me I'm sad you

MELISSA. But Jason gave me mine so it was ok.

MARNIE. Yeah but I'm

LINDA. Yeah.

MARNIE. Yeah.

(Pause.)

MELISSA. What's weird is We're all friends and none of us were engaged and then all of sudden all of us suddenly are Now.

That's the point. And what's different because we're engaged. Not me being upset.

(Pause.)

So then because we'd all got engaged and we all got our rings, we wanted to celebrate, so we went into the city. This was two months ago.

MARNIE. Kelly drove.

LINDA. She doesn't drink.

MARNIE. Right.

MELISSA. She has kids.

LINDA. Do you have a picture of Kelly?

MARNIE. Yeah. Yeah. Just a sec.

MELISSA. So Kelly drove

MARNIE. Here Look

(Shows large xerox photo of Kelly.)

And these are her kids.

(Shows a small photo of Kelly's kids.)

LINDA. They are so cute

MARNIE. I forgot to copy this one.

MELISSA. Kelly drove

MARNIE. Five of us went. Me, Melissa, Lori, Linda and Kelly. Kelly's already married and Lori well Lori well

LINDA. Do you have a picture of Lori?

MARNIE. Yeah.

(Unfolds, shows large xerox photo of Lori.)

This is the only picture I have of her.

LINDA. Lori probably won't get married

MARNIE. Yeah

MELISSA. I dunno

LINDA. No

MARNIE. Yeah

LINDA. Yeah Lori probably won't get married

MARNIE. She doesn't want to.

MELISSA. She might.

(To audience.)

We do everything together. The five of us.

MARNIE. But maybe.

MELISSA. She'll get married.

MARNIE. So Kelly drove

MELISSA. So we went into the city

LINDA. Just for the night To have fun

MARNIE. To celebrate

LINDA. Remember the

MARNIE. Yeah remember the

MELISSA. Yeah

ALL. Yeah yeah yeah yeah yeah

MELISSA. So we went into the city

LINDA. (*In spotlight. To the audience.*) The city's like a monster Like a sleeping dragon or some dark creature in the night that cracks open an eye, it just stares at you and dares you to come closer to it, to look down its dark streets, says "Come here" and whispers dark dangerous dark ideas into your ear It's fun It's fun it's I go into the city and I forget who I am, I forget to be afraid of anything, which, I don't know, I don't know how smart that is, but I know that when I'm in the city and I with my friends I just It's

MELISSA. We got drunk.

LINDA. Yeah.

MARNIE. Remember?

LINDA. Yeah.

(*They all laugh.*)

MELISSA. We were racing around like crazy. We went dancing and we were shouting and people were shouting at us and laughing and and Linda and Linda

LINDA. (*In a spotlight. To the audience.*) I've been reading about Hinduism at school. The Hindus They think They think the whole world is alive That everything That every flower every bit of wood and rock and the floating clouds And even the water that a small golden fish swims through Everything is living and feeling and

And that night I believed them I could see the world that they

I could see the city slowly opening its lazy dangerous eyes

They The Hindus They use their breath to slow down the tumbling hurdy gurdy of the world Slow it down so they can see the trees breathe, so they can fall in love with the wind, so they can

That night I could hear it I could hear the cement under my feet muttering, I could hear the streetlights arguing with me, I could hear a devil and an angel struggling grabbing at each other, young and old and

dead And I knew no one liked me and I knew
and then
I was dizzy and

MELISSA. Linda had too much to drink.

MARNIE. (*Smiles, nervous.*)

LINDA. Maybe

MELISSA. You had way too much. And she fainted. And Lori tried to catch her.

(*Pause.*)

And Lori broke her foot.

MARNIE. Yeah.

LINDA. I was fine.

MARNIE. Yeah but Lori

MELISSA. And I knew I knew that night
Cause there were cops and Lori was trying not to cry and that guy who ran the store And remember how your cell it didn't
I knew
What this ring means

(*Points at her wedding ring.*)

Is that there's a beautiful new path that we're all going to walk down. It's so It's beautiful
And it also means There's some places That's it We won't be going there any more. That's what's different now.

MARNIE. What?

MELISSA. What

MARNIE. You think that's true?

MELISSA. I'm sure it is. We're getting married.

MARNIE. Huh. Huh.

MELISSA. (*To audience.*) All I'm saying is: When you get engaged, don't go into the city. Don't go into the city.

MARNIE. Huh.

LINDA. I'm fine.

MELISSA. Show'm one more time.

> *(They all show their rings.)*

> Ok. That's it Let's go.

> **(MARNIE** *and* **LINDA** *exit,* **MELISSA** *turns just before exiting.)*

MELISSA. Don't go into the city.

> *(She exits.)*

> *(Music.)*

TWO.

(A sign or placard or heading:

OK SO FAST FORWARD: THREE WEEKS LATER. IN THE CITY.

Notes on this night in the Drunken City:

In every scene that follows, every character except Bob is drunk or tipsy, except during noted moments of clarity.

The city tilts when noted.

A city street late at night.)

EDDIE. *(Runs on from offstage right, stops halfway across stage. Yells back to offstage right.)*
Come on Come on!

(Runs offstage left.

Runs back onstage halfway. Yells back to offstage right.)
Come on Come on! Frank! Hurry it up!

(Runs offstage left.

Runs back onstage halfway. Stands.)
Let's go! Come on! Jeez!

(He tap-dances. Drunk. It is choreographed. Drunk. He is a good tap-dancer but he is drunk.

Yells offstage to **FRANK.***)*

EDDIE. Dude!

*(***FRANK** *enters.* **EDDIE** *taps.)*

FRANK. Eddie Shut up I'm trying to call Priscilla.

EDDIE. No.

FRANK. She isn't picking up her cellphone.

EDDIE. You promised me.

FRANK. What?

EDDIE. We're not talking about her. She broke up with you a year ago! And she doesn't even answer your texts anymore.

FRANK. That's why I'm calling her!

EDDIE. You're an idiot.

FRANK. Yeah? You're an idiot.

EDDIE. You're an idiot. I bring you out. I drive you here. I talk us into that club. I find you some girls.

FRANK. Yeah girls Some That one girl you wanted me to She kept squinting at me!

EDDIE. You're too picky.

FRANK. She was all Squint Squint Squint

EDDIE. She forgot her glasses! She told you that!

FRANK. At least Priscilla doesn't squint.

EDDIE. Frankie.

FRANK. She's probably out with that guy.

EDDIE. Frank. You gotta stop it with the thinking about Priscilla. She was a jerk.

FRANK. She wasn't a jerk.

EDDIE. She was. She dumped you. She strung you along and then she dumped you. She was a jerk.

FRANK. What do you know about it You're never in love

EDDIE. Hey you know I'm waiting. I told you I'm waiting I'm waiting for the right This doesn't have anything to do with me and me not

FRANK. Yeah. Well I was in love with Priscilla. So don't call her that. Because I don't like it.

(Awkward. Then:)

And anyway it was my fault she dumped me.

EDDIE. How?

FRANK. I didn't listen to her.

EDDIE. So?

FRANK. She kept saying things and I didn't listen to her. That's what she told me when I finally listened to her.

EDDIE. *(Mutters)* Yeah and she lied to you. About all that stuff!

FRANK. She only lied to me because I never listened to her. That's what she told me when I finally listened to her.

EDDIE. Frank.

FRANK. What?

EDDIE. Where're we going next?

FRANK. I'm going home.

EDDIE. Oh No no no my buddy. I'm taking you one more place. The girls are gorgeous.

FRANK. I'm tired Eddie. Gimme the keys to your car.

EDDIE. No. Why? No.

FRANK. You're not driving. You're drunk.

EDDIE. That other girl was into you.

FRANK. The squinter?

EDDIE. No, that other one before. I introduced you to her. We should of hung out with her.

FRANK. The girl with that thing on her neck?

EDDIE. She was checking you out and she said "who's that guy you're with" and I was "I'm not with him" and she was "no?" and I was "no, why?" and then she looked at me all

(Opens his eyes wide and cocks his head.)

FRANK. Why didn't you tell me?

EDDIE. I did. I was poking your arm and going

(Makes face.)

And then she said And then she said

FRANK. What?

EDDIE. And then she said

(Laughs.)

FRANK. You're drunk.

EDDIE. You're drunk Frankie.

FRANK. No you you're drunk Eddie.

EDDIE. You're drunk. Frank you're totally

FRANK. Eddie

EDDIE. I had a beer and a tequila shot. I'm not drunk. What are you saying Why are you saying that What are you saying?

FRANK. I had two shots.

EDDIE. Yeah Ok I had two shots too.

FRANK. No. You had four shots.

EDDIE. Yeah. So I had four shots. But that's it.

FRANK. And a beer.

EDDIE. And Ok a beer. Right. Big deal a beer.

FRANK. And another beer.

EDDIE. Two beers. Two. Pfft. Right.

FRANK. Yeah. Two beers.

EDDIE. And two shots.

FRANK. Four shots.

EDDIE. Four Shots.

FRANK. Four shots.

EDDIE. Yeah! (*Laughs.*) Two beers and four shots. That's it.

FRANK. At that bar.

EDDIE. I think I might of had a couple of margaritas. Didn't we have margaritas somewhere?

FRANK. (*Holds up his hand for the keys.*)

EDDIE. (*Gives them to him.*) I want another beer.

FRANK. Let's get out of here.

EDDIE. We could go back and see her.

FRANK. Who?

EDDIE. That girl with the thing on her neck

FRANK. I dunno That thing on her neck kinda made me anxious.

EDDIE. (*Tap-dances.*)

FRANK. She said something about me though?

EDDIE. Wanna go back?

FRANK. What'd she say?

EDDIE. I got something on my shoe.

FRANK. What?

EDDIE. What?

FRANK. What?

EDDIE. I got something on my shoe. I think it's gum. I fucking I hate when I get It's gum I think. It's gum.

(Sits on the ground.)

FRANK. What'd she say?

EDDIE. Who?

FRANK. *(Stands. Mouth open.)*

EDDIE. It is It's gum.

FRANK. I'm going home.

(**MELISSA, LINDA** *and* **MARNIE** *enter stage right.* **MARNIE** *wears a wedding veil. And a tiara.)*

LINDA. Whoo whoo!

MELISSA. She's getting married! She's getting married!

LINDA. Whoo whoo!

MELISSA & LINDA. Getting married!

LINDA. Whoo whoo! Married! Whoo whoo!

MARNIE. I'm getting married!

EDDIE. Hey She's getting married Frank.

FRANK. I know. I heard.

EDDIE. She's getting married!

LINDA. Whoo whoo!

EDDIE. You're getting married!

MARNIE. I know!

LINDA. You are!

(Starts crying.)

MARNIE. I know! I know!

MELISSA & LINDA. You are!

(Start crying.)

MELISSA. She's getting married!

MARNIE. I am! I am!

LINDA. I know! She is!

MELISSA & LINDA. She is!

MARNIE. I am!

THE DRUNKEN CITY 19

MELISSA. She's getting married!

(Wails.)

ALL THREE WOMEN. I know!

(Wail. Hug. Wail.)

FRANK. Why they crying?

MELISSA. Because she's getting married. Isn't that great?

(Cries.)

FRANK. I dunno.

EDDIE. Of course it's great.

FRANK. What's so great about getting married? Priscilla's probably gonna marry that guy.

EDDIE. Who's getting married?

LINDA. Shut up We just told you!

MARNIE. I am!

LINDA. And we're going to the wedding! Whoo whoo!

EDDIE. Who's going to the wedding?

LINDA. Shut up We just told you!

MELISSA. We are! We're in it!

EDDIE. Who's in it?

LINDA. We just told you! Shut up!

EDDIE. I got gum on my shoe.

MARNIE. You do?

LINDA. Guys! Guys! Check your shoes! Check your shoes for gum!

(The women all sit. They check for gum.)

LINDA. NO GUM!

MARNIE. NO GUM!

MELISSA. NO GUM!

LINDA. Alright!

MARNIE. I'm Marnie. I'm getting married.

FRANK. Why?

MARNIE. I dunno. What d'ya mean?

MELISSA & LINDA. We're her bridesmaids!

LINDA. Bridesmaids rule! Whoo whoo!

EDDIE. I'm a dentist.

LINDA. You are?

EDDIE. And I can tap-dance.

(Tap-dances.)

LINDA. Look! Man! How'd you learn to Look Marnie! Look! Look!

EDDIE. Who are you marrying?

MARNIE. Some guy.

MELISSA & LINDA. Marnie!

(Laughing.)

MARNIE. Some guy I

LINDA. His name's Gary!

MARNIE. Pipe it down Linda!

LINDA. *(Loud whisper:)* His name's Gary.

MELISSA. *(Loud whisper:)* He's really nice!

EDDIE. How nice?

LINDA. *(Loud whisper:)* He's nice and his name's Gary!

MELISSA. *(Loud whisper:)* He's really nice! He is! He's a nice guy!

LINDA. *(Loud whisper:)* He's got a nice ass! Whoo whoo!

EDDIE. *(Loud whisper:)* Alrighty there! Whoo whoo!

MELISSA. Linda!

LINDA. He does!

MARNIE. He does.

MELISSA. It's true he does He's got a nice ass!

(They all laugh.)

FRANK. What's your name again?

MARNIE. You're drunk.

FRANK. Yeah.

(Smiles.)

MARNIE. I'm Marnie. I'm a bride-to-be. And I'm a princess. I got a tiara. See? We were at the loudest bar. I could barely hear myself think. We had pink drinks.

LINDA. I drank a lot of'm.

MELISSA. What's your name?

FRANK. Frank. He's Eddie.

MELISSA. Frank. That's a cute name. You're cute. He's cute Linda.

MARNIE. Wait a minute I know you You work at my bank.

FRANK. That'd probably be me.

MELISSA. You're from our town?

FRANK. We both are.

MARNIE. He works at my bank!

LINDA. He does?

MELISSA. Which one? The one over on?

MARNIE. Yeah. My bank!

MELISSA. His name's Frank?

MARNIE. Yeah!

MELISSA. His name is Frank.

MARNIE & MELISSA. And he works at my/your bank! His name is Frank and

LINDA. At a bank At a bank at a bank bank bank

FRANK. Ok. Let's get out of here Eddie.

MARNIE. No come on! We're joking!

MELISSA. We're just joking Frank.

LINDA. Mr. Bank Man!

MARNIE. Come on.

MELISSA. We were just. Come on.

MARNIE. You're my banker and I wanna meet you.

MELISSA. I want you to be my banker too.

LINDA. Me too.

FRANK. Eddie.

EDDIE. They wanna meet you Frankie.

LINDA. We got bridesmaids dresses today.

MELISSA. Except her. She's gonna wear a gown.

LINDA. A GOWN.

MELISSA. And it is FANCY.

EDDIE. How fancy?

MARNIE. It's fancy.

MELISSA. Frank. You're cute. You got a girlfriend?

EDDIE. No he doesn't.

MELISSA & LINDA. Huh.

MELISSA. Really. You're cute.

LINDA. It's all white.

EDDIE. What?

LINDA. Her gown. Ours're blue.

MELISSA. Yeah.

LINDA. Melissa looks good in blue.

MELISSA. I do.

EDDIE. I bet you do.

LINDA. She does Frank.

MELISSA. I do. And today Frank we got gloves.

EDDIE. Even nicer!

LINDA. I've got short arms.

EDDIE. You do?

MARNIE. You do not!

FRANK. Lemme see.

LINDA. Look.

MELISSA. Lori and Marnie and me and Linda and Kelly all went to the bride store today and got gloves. They're satin.

LINDA. My gloves go all the way up to my armpits!

MELISSA. They do not!

MARNIE. Your arms are fine.

MELISSA. Kelly's the one who's got Kelly's got short arms.

LINDA. Yeah she does!

EDDIE. Who's Kelly?

LINDA. Poor Kelly.

MELISSA. It's me I'm Melissa It's me and Lori and Linda and Marnie and Kelly Kelly Kelly Kelly is one of the bridesmaids too well she's the matron and she has really short arms If you think Linda's arms are short, you should see Kelly's

LINDA. Yeah Yeah Yeah Poor Kelly

MELISSA. When we got the gloves we all put them on and then Kelly put hers on
And then

(Opens eyes wide.)

LINDA. Whoa.

MELISSA. No one said anything We couldn't even look at Kelly We were just looking down at the ground

LINDA. Like this.

MELISSA. I never noticed that Her arms are so short.

LINDA. Me neither!

MARNIE. Me neither!

MELISSA. She's gonna have to get her gloves shortened!

LINDA. It's expensive being a bridesmaid. Especially when you're shaped funny.

FRANK. You have nice arms.

MARNIE. Thanks. Really? Thanks.

*(**MARNIE** and **FRANK** sneak a kiss.)*

EDDIE. Where are Kelly and Lori?

MELISSA. Kelly had to go home

ALL THREE WOMEN. She has kids.

MARNIE. And Lori's foot was throbbing.

*(**MELISSA** and **MARNIE** point at **LINDA**.)*

MELISSA. I wanna be a bride. I'm never going to be a bride!

MARNIE. You will be.

LINDA. Sure you're gonna be a bride someday.

MELISSA. She's getting this great wedding With everything It's gonna be awesome Everything's all set and waiting and everyone is so psyched for her it's gonna be awesome It's a huge huge huge huge moment in her life and it's gonna be awesome and then she gets to start out a whole new life and everything.

EDDIE. You'll get married. You're pretty.

MELISSA. Thank you.

EDDIE. Isn't she pretty Frank?

FRANK. Yeah.

LINDA. She broke up with her boyfriend.

MELISSA. Linda shut up!

LINDA. Well you did.

MELISSA. I had to!

EDDIE. Frank broke up with his girlfriend too.

MELISSA. You did? You did Frank?

MARNIE. You did huh?

FRANK. Nice Eddie.

EDDIE. Frankie you gotta get over her.

FRANK. She broke up with me.

MARNIE. How come?

FRANK. Her name was Priscilla She was just this girl

MELISSA. She was stupid. You're cute. My ex is rotten!

EDDIE. He is?

LINDA. He fooled around on her. Twice!

(*MARNIE and* **FRANK** *sneak a kiss.*)

MELISSA. I forgave him the first time.

EDDIE. You did?

MELISSA. We were engaged!

LINDA. She shouldn't of made him come back to her.

MELISSA. But then

LINDA. Cause he did it again.

MELISSA. Marriage is SACRED! He gave me a RING! I had a RING!

(*MARNIE and* **FRANK** *are kissing. They've been sneaking kisses for a bit without being noticed.*

LINDA, *and then* MELISSA *and then* EDDIE, *all see them. The city tilts. They all stumble.)*

LINDA. Whoa!

MELISSA. Marnie!

EDDIE. Frank!

(Pause. Open mouths.)

EDDIE. Man dude!

*(*MARNIE *and* FRANK *kiss again. The city tilts. They all stumble.)*

MELISSA. Marnie stop it!

LINDA. Whoa!

MELISSA. What are you doing?

EDDIE. What're you doing Frank?

MARNIE. What?

MELISSA. You can't you can't you can't You can't kiss some guy at your bachelorette party, Gary's gonna kill us.

MARNIE. I can kiss him if I want to. I'm not married yet.

MELISSA. No you can't!

LINDA. You can't Marnie!

*(*MARNIE *is about to kiss* FRANK *again.)*

MELISSA. Marnie!

EDDIE. You can't kiss her!

MARNIE. He's fun to kiss! He's got soft lips.

FRANK. I do?

MARNIE. Gary doesn't have soft lips. He has hard lips.

FRANK. I have soft lips Eddie.

MELISSA. Stop kissing her!

FRANK. OW!

MARNIE. Don't hit him!

LINDA. Melissa!

MELISSA. He's gonna ruin everything!

FRANK. Ow! Ow! Jeez Louise!

   (Laughing)

   Pull her off of me Eddie!

EDDIE. Man.

FRANK. OW!

   (Not laughing.)

   That frickin HURT! JEEZ!

MARNIE. Melissa! Melissa!

FRANK. OW!

LINDA. Melissa's going crazy.

MELISSA. He's gonna he's gonna he's gonna

MARNIE. Melissa cut it out!

EDDIE. Hey hey hey HEY. HEY.

   (Pause.)

FRANK. Ow. Ow.

MELISSA. *(Panting. To audience.)* This is how things get
   ruined. This is how things unravel and fall apart. This
   is how all of a sudden no one's smiling any more, why
   people end up standing around embarrassed and sad.

EDDIE. *(To audience. Opens mouth.)*

LINDA. *(To audience.)* I drink too much. The world scares
   me.

MELISSA. *(In a spot. To audience.*

   During this, **FRANK** *and* **MARNIE** *sneak off-stage.)*

   I had everything. I had a ring. It was such a beautiful
   night the night Jason gave it to me. My hair was up like
   And Jason looked so shiny and redfaced and he was
   smiling at me like I was the only person anywhere anywhere anywhere. It was gonna be awesome. And. And
   we were going to buy a house. I'd already picked it out.
   It had a gazebo in the backyard. With screens. Where
   you could put a table in the summer.

   Then slowly Like a murmur that I didn't notice at first
   I couldn't hear it properly I kept hearing these two
   names. These two names over and over in different low
   voices. Jason and Jessica. Jessica and Jason.

What kind of name is Jessica anyways Who'd name their kid that? Jessica It's a stupid name.

It was humiliating. I gave my ring back to Jason. And suddenly all over again I had nothing all over again.

(Blinks.)

MELISSA. Where are they?

EDDIE. I dunno.

LINDA. Who?

MELISSA. Marnie and that stupid guy!

LINDA. Oh my god where'd they go?

MELISSA. We have to find them. Gary's gonna kill us Linda.

EDDIE. *(Muttering:)* Frank's not stupid.

MELISSA. What?

EDDIE. Frank's not stupid.

MELISSA. My friend Marnie and my friend Gary have planned a very beautiful very spiritual very They're getting married. In a church! They bought a car. And Gary's been talking about getting a dog. A miniature schnauzer which is the kind of dog that's very good with children so you can guess what else he's been thinking about.

LINDA. Children!

MELISSA. And now because Kelly and Linda wanted to have a bachelorette party

LINDA. I knew it was gonna be fun.

MELISSA. Linda!

LINDA. What?

MELISSA. This is as bad as last time we came here and you broke Lori's foot!

LINDA. Melissa!

MELISSA. Worse!

LINDA. You're

MELISSA. And now because we brought Marnie out and she kissed your stupid friend

EDDIE. (*Mutters.*)

MELISSA. My friend Gary's gonna be really really really really really mad at us and there's gonna be heck to pay! I'm calling Bob.

EDDIE. Who's Bob?

MELISSA. He'll talk some sense into Marnie.

LINDA. Maybe we should call Gary.

MELISSA. We can't call Gary. He'll kill us.

EDDIE. This Gary guy doesn't sound so great.

MELISSA. He is too great He's a great guy. He is. You don't know what you're talking about.

LINDA. Melissa used to date him before Marnie.

MELISSA. Shut up Linda!

EDDIE. Really?

LINDA. I want another a those pink drinks.

MELISSA. This city's drunk! We should have never come back here for this frickin' party!

We're going to find them. Then someone's gonna talk some sense into Marnie. Or I'm gonna kill her. Or I'm gonna kill him. Or I'm gonna kill both of them.

EDDIE. I think I'll wait here.

MELISSA. No you won't. He won't Linda. He won't. Hey.

EDDIE. But.

MELISSA. You're coming with us.

EDDIE. But.

MELISSA. Hey. Hey.

LINDA. I have to pee Melissa.

MELISSA. We'll find you a bathroom. Ok come on let's go.

(*Stomps off, followed by* **LINDA** *and* **EDDIE.**

Then, music: the sound of flowers and candy at night.

On the corner of Second and Baxter.

FRANK *and* **MARNIE** *enter. They kiss. They kiss. They wander.* **FRANK** *pulls* **MARNIE** *towards him to kiss her again.*)

MARNIE. Listen to that.

FRANK. What?

MARNIE. It's quiet. It's so quiet.

FRANK. You're pretty.

MARNIE. SH!

(She listens.)

It's been so noisy around me for so long. I haven't been able to think. Don't say anything for a second just for a

(She kisses him to quiet him.

She listens.)

It's so quiet.

FRANK. *(Kisses her.)*

MARNIE. You're kissing me too loud!

FRANK. Sorry.

MARNIE. It's just Ever since Gary asked me to marry him it's been so noisy everywhere.

FRANK. People get excited.

MARNIE. Do they ever. It's crazy. It's crazy.

FRANK. You're pretty.

MARNIE. Once anyone hears about it, I feel them, everybody, people, they're crazy, they hear I'm getting married and they look at me and it's like, it's, almost, they look at me and their eyes bug out, they see what they want and then they get really noisy.
You ever been engaged?

FRANK. No. I was gonna be but.

MARNIE. What happened?

FRANK. It was that girl Priscilla.

MARNIE. Oh.

FRANK. Yeah. She didn't

MARNIE. Well it's hard.

FRANK. I thought it'd be fun.

MARNIE. No it's hard. People start watching you.

FRANK. Huh.

MARNIE. And Oh this is screwed up Frank I call my best friends I call up Melissa or Linda or Kelly and they say "How's it going?" and I say "Fine" and they shout into the phone "You're engaged!" and I go "I know! I know!" and Linda goes "Whoo whoo!" but at the same time in my journal I've been writing things, but everything just keeps going forward, my Mom is all "The invitations are printed! Honey! The invitations! Look! Look!" and I'm all "They look great Mom!" and she looks so happy.

FRANK. (*Kisses her. Kisses her again.*)

MARNIE. I've been unhappy about something but. And.

FRANK. Why didn't you talk to anyone?

MARNIE. Who am I gonna tell?

FRANK. Isn't there someone you could

MARNIE. Last week?

FRANK. (*Kisses her. Kisses her again.*)

MARNIE. My Dad

My Dad and I were upstairs wrapping birthday presents for my nephew and my niece, they're twins, they're so cute, they both have noses that

(*Pushes her nose.*)

Cute. Cute. They are cute.

So we were upstairs and we were wrapping their presents and my Dad says "How're you doing?" and I burst into tears. I was just. And.

And I tried to explain it to him I said "Dad Gary ties his ties too tight." and he said "Uh huh?" and I said "Really really tight" and he looked at me He's such a nice guy my Dad Do you like your Dad?

FRANK. Yeah. I do.

MARNIE. Me too. I love my Dad. My Dad looked at me and I wanted to say "I think I might have made a mistake I might have" but I was scared because he likes Gary and they both have Toyota Corollas and they both like watching TV together and my Dad's so happy I'm marrying someone like him. I didn't want to disappoint him.

I'm so mad at myself I couldn't tell him the truth.

FRANK. Sometimes it's scary to be honest.

MARNIE. I don't know how to be.

FRANK. You don't?

MARNIE. No.

FRANK. Maybe you could practice.

MARNIE. Sometimes, I know I should, I have to say something, but then I don't.

FRANK. It's important to learn how to be honest.

MARNIE. When Gary asked me to marry him we were at our favorite restaurant It's Italian and it's really loud and by mistake I said yes. I don't think I was really listening. I think maybe I was thinking about something else. And he put the ring on my finger

FRANK. You have beautiful hands.

MARNIE. I bite my fingernails.

FRANK. Your fingers are beautiful.

MARNIE. I dunno Frank. I go to my nail lady her name's Sondra and I swear sometimes she looks at my hands and she turns to this other nail lady Lucy and they say all these things in Vietnamese.

FRANK. Every single one of your fingers

(Kisses each finger on one hand.)

MARNIE. I've got to figure this out.

FRANK. Maybe you don't want to marry him.

MARNIE. Everybody would kill me.

FRANK. My sister she's always saying "A girl's got a right to change her mind." That's what she says "A girl's got a right to change her mind."

MARNIE. You're so nice to me.

FRANK. Well

MARNIE. He makes the bed, and then he leaves his socks

on the floor!

FRANK. Huh.

MARNIE. I know huh. And his shoes!

FRANK. His shoes too?

MARNIE. Yes!

FRANK. Huh.

MARNIE. I know! It's one sock over here and there's one over here! On the floor!

FRANK. That's terrible!

MARNIE. It is!

FRANK. Call the cops!

MARNIE. Frank!

FRANK. (*Siren noise.*)

MARNIE. Cut it out!

FRANK. (*Explosion noise.*)

MARNIE. I get up in the night and his shoes and I'm clunk clunk clunk and tripping I'm just trying to walk to the bathroom!

And he won't clean his car. It's completely full of crap!

FRANK. So what if his car's a mess?

MARNIE. It's a car full of crap!

FRANK. My car's a mess.

MARNIE. Nobody wants to marry a messy man.

FRANK. Really?

MARNIE. Nope.

FRANK. I didn't know that.

MARNIE. And now he wants me to clean it up. He wants me to clean up his car. Because we're getting married suddenly he thinks I'm. I don't know what I'm going to do. I don't I just I'm I

FRANK. Ok ok ok. Ok. Ok. Ok.

MARNIE. I'm.

FRANK. Ok ok it's ok.

MARNIE. And I don't think I don't I can't tell anyone. I don't think I can.

FRANK. It's ok. Hey. You told me.

MARNIE. I don't even know you. How would I tell my Mom? She's just going to tell me to clean up his car. How would I tell Melissa?

FRANK. It'll be ok.

MARNIE. I know I know Just give me a second. Lemme alone for a second.

FRANK. Ok.

MARNIE. Ok?

FRANK. Yeah of course.

MARNIE. Thanks.

FRANK. Wait here for a second.

> (**FRANK** *exits.*
>
> **MARNIE** *waits.*
>
> **FRANK** *enters. Hands* **MARNIE** *a donut.*)

MARNIE. Gary doesn't like it when I eat donuts.

FRANK. Gary's not here.

MARNIE. I've always been a liar. I've got to stop lying.

> (**EDDIE** *and* **LINDA** *enter. They're drinking beers.*)

EDDIE. Hi Frank.

FRANK. Hey Eddie.

LINDA. Hey Marnie.

MARNIE. Hi Linda.

EDDIE. Hey.

MARNIE. Hi.

FRANK. Hi.

LINDA. Hi.

MARNIE. Where's Melissa?

LINDA. She's out looking for you. We were slowing her down.

MARNIE. Yeah?

EDDIE. She went to her car to get a map.

LINDA. She wants to make a comprehensive plan to find

you guys.

MARNIE. Huh.

LINDA. Yeah.

EDDIE. She's very determined.

LINDA. Yeah.

FRANK. Yeah?

EDDIE. Oh yeah.

LINDA. I should probably call her. Since we already found you.

MARNIE. No Linda. Don't. Ok? Don't?

(Pause.)

LINDA. So how's it going?

FRANK. Good. Right?

MARNIE. Yeah. Good.

LINDA. Oh. Good.

EDDIE. Great.

(Pause.

FRANK *and* **MARNIE** *kiss.)*

LINDA. Oh you guys are still kissing.

MARNIE. Yeah.

FRANK. Yeah.

LINDA. Oh.

EDDIE. Oh.

(Pause.)

LINDA. Melissa's not gonna like that.

EDDIE. No.

LINDA. No.

Lucky she went to get the map.

EDDIE. Yeah

MARNIE. Yeah!

FRANK. Yeah!

LINDA. You think you should be still kissing him?

MARNIE. Yeah.

FRANK. Yeah.

LINDA. Huh. Because well because. All your friends, Melissa, me, Lori, Kelly, Bob, the whole group of us, we all All of us promised we'd help you get married. I don't think you should be kissing him.

MARNIE. I'm not going to hold you to that promise.

LINDA. But then when it's my turn with Jack how am I gonna be able to count on you?

MARNIE. I might not want to get married.

LINDA. What?

EDDIE. Oh man!

LINDA. What?

MARNIE. I was thinking

LINDA. Oh my god.

EDDIE. Frank

MARNIE. I'm just thinking

LINDA. Oh my god. Oh my god. Oh my god. Oh my god.

FRANK. Take it easy.

EDDIE. Oh sure. How's she gonna take it easy?

FRANK. She can just relax.

EDDIE. Her friend's all messed up.

MARNIE. Who you calling?

LINDA. Bob.

MARNIE. Oh no don't call Bob.

LINDA. I have to.

MARNIE. He's probably asleep.

LINDA. Too late Melissa already called him!

FRANK. Who's Bob?

LINDA. You should leave her alone!

MARNIE. Linda.

FRANK. Who's Bob?

EDDIE. They all planned the whole wedding. She told me all about it. They all worked on it together. It's got a whole country classic theme!

LINDA. I'm doing the flowers! With straw! And acorns!

EDDIE. They're having a barn dance!

FRANK. Who's Bob?

EDDIE. He's making the cake.

FRANK. A country classic cake?

LINDA. Yes!

MARNIE. He's gonna be mad.

LINDA. I've had enough of this Marnie. Go home and apologize to Gary, or better yet, lie to him, or not say anything.

MARNIE. Don't wake Bob up.

LINDA. You're talking to him.

MARNIE. I don't want to talk to him. He's going to be mad at me too.

LINDA. Everyone's going to be mad at you. You better get used to it.

MARNIE. See? See? I told you I told you they'd all be.

FRANK. Hey. Ease up on her.

LINDA. (On cellphone:) Bob? Yeah.

MARNIE. I'm not talking to him!

LINDA. (To EDDIE:) Where are we?

MARNIE. Why?

EDDIE. On the corner of Second and Baxter.

LINDA. (On cellphone:) On the corner of Second and Baxter. Second and Baxter. Second and Baxter. And Baxter.

MARNIE. Just a He's coming here? Frank.

LINDA. (Whispered on cellphone:) Hurry up. Ok.

MARNIE. Where is he? Frank.

FRANK. It's ok.

LINDA. He says Stop kissing.

MARNIE. Is he with Melissa?

LINDA. You guys can't be kissing when he gets here. Just pretend you aren't at least ok?

MARNIE. Let's get out of here. Come on Frank. Let go my arm Linda.

FRANK. Let go her arm.

LINDA. You stop it.

EDDIE. Frankie.

FRANK. What?

EDDIE. Dude! They're having a hayride!

FRANK. She's really pretty.

MARNIE. See how sweet he is?

LINDA. Why can't you leave her alone? Marnie!

FRANK. I like her.

LINDA. Hold on to them. Eddie! Make them stay here! Marnie!

(On cellphone:)

Melissa! Get over here quick!

MARNIE. Let go of me Linda!

LINDA. Marnie! Melissa! Marnie!

MARNIE. Let go!

(MARNIE and FRANK exit.)

LINDA. Eddie why didn't you hold them?

EDDIE. You wanted me to grab at them?

LINDA. Yes! You're no help at all!

(Exiting, on cellphone:)

I had 'em I had'em But they're getting away! I'm following them!

MELISSA. *(Offstage, on cellphone:)* Don't lose them!

Bob she's got them!

Don't lose them Linda!

(BOB and MELISSA enter.)

Where are they? Where are they?

EDDIE. Linda went that way.

MELISSA. *(On cellphone:)* What? What? Oh goddamn crap!

EDDIE. Hi.

BOB. Uh huh.

LINDA. (*Enters, on cellphone:*) I lost them.

(**LINDA** *and* **MELISSA** *shut cellphones.*)

I lost them. Hi Bob. I don't know, they just, they scooted and I lost them. I'm sorry.

MELISSA. Crap.

EDDIE. Hi.

MELISSA. Crap!

LINDA. He didn't even try to help me stop them.

EDDIE. You're handsome.

BOB. Who are you? Who's he? Who are you?

MELISSA. He's Eddie. He's the jerk's friend.

EDDIE. (*Mutters.*)

MELISSA. He is too a jerk!

BOB. You guys are all drunk.

LINDA. They had these really pretty pink drinks that sparkled.

MELISSA. Doesn't matter. We have a situation Bob.

LINDA. We do. Marnie's gone crazy.

BOB. Who are you?

EDDIE. I'm Eddie. Hi.

BOB. You're all drunk.

EDDIE. (*Mutters.*)

BOB. You are.

MELISSA. Bob.

BOB. How come you guys didn't invite me to the bachelorette party?

LINDA. You're a guy.

BOB. Yeah so? I might wanna get married one of these days.

LINDA. Oh yeah right.

MELISSA. Bob we have a situation.

BOB. I might.

LINDA. You wouldn't of worn the tiara. You have to wear

the tiara to come to the party.

BOB. I woulda worn it.

LINDA. Oh yeah.

MELISSA. We gotta make a real plan.

BOB. Ok let's figure this thing out. But I'm gonna talk to you two about this not inviting me thing later. It kind of pisses me off.

LINDA. Don't threaten me Bob.

BOB. I'm not threatening you. I'm just mad you guys didn't

MELISSA. Come on Bob, focus.

LINDA. Bob's good at planning. He'll figure this out. He was in the army.

BOB. I was in the Marines.

MELISSA. Focus.

LINDA. Yeah yeah the Marines.

BOB. There's a difference Linda.

LINDA. Yeah yeah.

BOB. There is!

MELISSA. Bob!

BOB. Ok.

MELISSA. Where would he take her?

EDDIE. Don't scream at me.

BOB. We should split up.

LINDA. Good idea Bob. See? I told you.

MELISSA. Think!

EDDIE. Stop it!

BOB. And we should find them and then bring them back here.

LINDA. Yeah! Good idea Bob.

MELISSA. Think!

EDDIE. I don't have to think, I know what he's going to do.

MELISSA. What?

EDDIE. Frank's gonna bring her back here.

MELISSA. That's stupid.

LINDA. That is stupid. Isn't that stupid Bob?

BOB. What makes you think he'll do that?

EDDIE. Because that's my car. He has my keys.

BOB. Oh.

MELISSA. Oh.

LINDA. Oh.

EDDIE. So we should wait here.

LINDA. We can't just wait here.

MELISSA. We'll split up.

LINDA. Good idea.

EDDIE. I'm staying here.

LINDA. I'm not staying with him this time. He's like a lump. He doesn't even grab people when you tell him to.

MELISSA. I'm not staying with him.

LINDA. Well I'm not staying with him.

MELISSA. Well I'm not staying with him either.

LINDA. Melissa!

MELISSA. Linda!

LINDA. Bob!

BOB. Fine. You two go.

LINDA. Oh. Good idea. Ok. Ok!

MELISSA. Ok.

BOB. I'll stay with him so if anything.

MELISSA. Ok. Check.

LINDA. Come on Come on!

   (*Runs offstage left.*)

BOB. I'll call you if anything.

MELISSA. Ok. Check.

LINDA. (*Runs back onstage.*) Come on Come on! Melissa! Hurry it up!

   (*Runs offstage left.*)

BOB. And you keep your cellphones out and call us if anything.

MELISSA. Ok. Check.

LINDA. (*Runs back onstage. Stands.*) Let's go! Come on! Jeez!

MELISSA. Ok ok. Ok!

(**MELISSA** *and* **LINDA** *run off.*)

EDDIE. Ok so your friends?

BOB. I know.

EDDIE. They're.

BOB. They're all wound up.

EDDIE. Yeah well. Kinda!

BOB. Yeah well your friend

EDDIE. What?

BOB. Your friend's screwing up our friend's life.

EDDIE. No.

BOB. Yes.

EDDIE. No. Your friend is screwing up her own life.

BOB. Yeah?

EDDIE. Yeah. So don't

BOB. So don't what?

EDDIE. (*Mutters:*) She could do a lot worse than Frank.

BOB. What?

EDDIE. (*Mutters:*) That Gary guy doesn't sound

BOB. It's Melissa.

EDDIE. That one.

BOB. She's got a broken heart.

EDDIE. Frank's a good guy.

BOB. This guy she loved, Jason, what a dick he was and we all knew it but love, you know, you gotta let people do what they're gonna do right? So Melissa. I hear about Jason and this Jessica girl and I think "oh no" and then Melissa comes running into work and shows me her ring and she was so excited.

So we watch out for each other.

EDDIE. (*Mutters:*) He's not like that.

BOB. What?

EDDIE. At least wait til you meet Frank before you judge him.

BOB. Marnie's engaged.

EDDIE. Seems like she's getting cold feet.

BOB. Seems like he should leave her alone.

EDDIE. I'm psyched he's. A year ago his girlfriend Priscilla she was finished with him and ever since he's been He mopes. He hasn't done anything. So I'm kinda psyched he's all.

BOB. Some devil's taken over Marnie's body. Marnie's never done anything like this. This is something Linda'd do.

EDDIE. (*Laughs.*)

BOB. But not Marnie.

EDDIE. Not Frank either. You should have seen him.
    They're both acting crazy.

BOB. Yeah.

EDDIE. Right?

BOB. Running around like a couple of kids.

EDDIE. Right?

BOB. Making everyone else scream and shout!

EDDIE. I know.

BOB. Crazy.

EDDIE. I know huh.

BOB. Would you ever act like that?

EDDIE. Me? No. No. No. No. Would you?

BOB. Me? No. Me neither.

EDDIE. No.

BOB. Because it's crazy right?

EDDIE. Yeah. Yeah.

    (*Pause.*)

    Love's strange though. You can fall in love just like that.

BOB. No you can't.

EDDIE. Yeah you can.

BOB. Just like that? Boom?

EDDIE. Haven't you ever seen someone and just thought "I've got to get a lot closer to that person and ask them a whole lotta questions"?

BOB. No.

EDDIE. Come on.

BOB. Do you go up to someone like that and ask them questions?

EDDIE. No. But Frank's always saying I should. I always

BOB. You always protect your friend like this?

EDDIE. He's my friend.

BOB. I like it.

EDDIE. Well.

BOB. I think I know why Marnie's freaking out. I'm not any good at any of this frickin love crap either. I've had a bunch of boyfriends and none of them have worked out So I can't pretend I know what I'm doing.

EDDIE. No one does.

BOB. But I do know the whole thing's hard. She's probably scared.

EDDIE. I would be. Getting married.

BOB. It's scary.

EDDIE. Yeah.

BOB. Love.

EDDIE. Yeah. Love.

BOB. Yeah. So.

EDDIE. I like that ring.

BOB. What?

EDDIE. That

BOB. This one? It's just silver.

EDDIE. So's mine.

BOB. Here.

(*They exchange rings.*)

EDDIE. I like all these little patterny things.

BOB. Yeah they're

EDDIE. I like how they

BOB. This one's pretty simple.

EDDIE. Yeah I

BOB. It's kinda

EDDIE. I saw it and I liked it, because it's so plain.

BOB. Yeah it's plain.

EDDIE. You think it's too plain?

BOB. Huh. It fits.

EDDIE. (*Tries on Bob's ring.*)

BOB. I got that one in Mexico. After my last boyfriend
  When he broke up with me I bought it for myself.
  I had to buy it for myself. I was in Mexico. And he
  wasn't in love with me any more Because he got lost in
  the relationship Because I must have done something.
  That's the reason I'm sick of love. It's too hard.

EDDIE. It's not so hard.

BOB. It is.

EDDIE. I think love's easy. It's waiting for it that's hard.

BOB. I meet a guy and at first he's himself with me. He
  kisses me because he wants to and it's fun He's push-
  ing himself all up against me and I get to push back
  and it's fun He's trying his tricks he's got all his tricks
  going and he's juggling and joking and that makes me
  laugh and it's fun
  and then
  all of a sudden He falls in love and suddenly it's all
  "let's put candles in the bathroom" and "I think I'm
  in love" and

  (*He makes googoo eyes. *)

EDDIE. You don't like candles?

BOB. And then he forgets who he is. And he gets mad at me
  for that. And says it's because I'm too hard on him.

EDDIE. I'm always getting dizzy. When I'm in love.

BOB. So I'm "Forget about it."

EDDIE. Huh.

BOB. Enough's enough. I'm done with it. And it's ok. It's good. I'm ok. I work hard. I like working. I love my job. That's what I love.

EDDIE. Huh.

BOB. They all work at my bakery with me. On Oak Street. Near Carlyle Park? Melissa said you're from our town You ever been to my bakery?

EDDIE. What's it called?

BOB. The Sunshine Bakery.

EDDIE. Really?

BOB. It was called that when I bought it.

EDDIE. All those girls do?

BOB. Yeah.

EDDIE. Even that Melissa girl?

BOB. She's a hard worker. And she's loyal.

EDDIE. Uh huh.

BOB. Well not Linda. She doesn't work with us. But she comes and eats a lot of muffins. But Lori and Marnie and Melissa do. And Kelly doesn't. She has kids. Linda's at divinity school. She's studying to be a minister.

EDDIE. She is?

BOB. She's only in her first year.

EDDIE. Yeah.

BOB. Well.

EDDIE. You'd never think of her as a.

BOB. You're a dentist and you tap-dance. You'd never think.

EDDIE. How'd you know that?

BOB. What?

EDDIE. That I tap-dance.

BOB. Well.

EDDIE. Huh?

BOB. That's what Melissa

EDDIE. What?

BOB. She said you.

EDDIE. She did huh?

BOB. Do you?

EDDIE. What?

BOB. Tap-dance?

EDDIE. No. Sometimes.

BOB. Show me some.

EDDIE. What? Oh. I don't know. Naw.

BOB. Come on.

EDDIE. Naw I'm. That's ok no.

BOB. Come on.

EDDIE. I don't just tap-dance for everyone.

BOB. Oh.

EDDIE. I didn't mean

BOB. Sure.

(*Pause.*)

EDDIE. I didn't mean

BOB. Forget it. It's ok.

(*During this next section of the play* **BOB** *and* **EDDIE** *sit watching the road. Eddie blacks out for a moment. Looks vague. They sit.*

On another street. **MARNIE** *and* **FRANK** *enter. They are entering a church. Alone. Sweet, dim light.*)

FRANK. How's this?

MARNIE. Are you sure we should be in here?

FRANK. This is one of the last churches in the city that doesn't lock its doors at night In case someone's in trouble I figure we're in trouble right?

MARNIE. I've never been in a church in the middle of the night.

FRANK. I figured you want it quiet.

MARNIE. It's beautiful.

FRANK. Look at the.

MARNIE. Gary would laugh.

FRANK. Why?

MARNIE. I don't like going to church with him. He starts sitting up straight.

FRANK. You wanna get out of here?

MARNIE. No. I like it here with you. Stop it Don't kiss me!

FRANK. Why not?

MARNIE. It's church!

FRANK. So?

MARNIE. Jesus is right there!

FRANK. He doesn't mind.

MARNIE. Frank be serious.

FRANK. I am. He's up there smiling at us.

MARNIE. I'm not kissing you in a church. I got more important things to figure out. Be serious.

FRANK. You were going to kiss Gary in a church.

MARNIE. You gotta help me figure this out. Please?

FRANK. Why'd you even tell him yes?

MARNIE. I wanted the wedding.

FRANK. What? That's just

MARNIE. Because it's gonna be a gorgeous wedding. I'm gonna wear my Mom's wedding dress

it's from 1910 and her Mom wore it

and her mom's mom wore it

and it's satin with inlaid pearls, well not inlaid pearls, that's not the word I'm, and I remember when I was a tiny girl I remember thinking "I gonna wear that dress" because it's the most, it's gorgeous and I'm gonna get to be looked at, I'm gonna,

Gary was just a prop. He was. He was just

And I knew he wanted me to say yes, so I did. I just

I kept lying

And then, worse, Frank, worse, he suddenly he he changed on me.

FRANK. How?

MARNIE. He started acting like a husband. How he thinks a husband is, the world's dangerous and he has to protect me and that means I have to listen to him and he's gonna tell me what to do and I'm gonna have to act like he tells me. He's gonna be like his Dad. But his Mom's this little mousy woman who never says Boo. And I'm not gonna be her.

Uh uh.

But I just don't know what to say to Gary.

FRANK. Make something up.

MARNIE. I want to tell him the truth. I do.

FRANK. Well then tell it.

MARNIE. It's good you brought me here. I'm gonna need some help doing all this. Will you wait for me?

FRANK. Of course I will.

MARNIE. I'm gonna go sit and be quiet for a minute. You're so sweet. I wish I'd met you before I met Gary.

(She goes offstage to the altar.

FRANK *waits. We can see* **BOB, EDDIE** *and* **FRANK** *all waiting onstage.)*

LINDA. *(To audience:)* Sometimes I wake up in the morning, I'm so lonely. Jack's already out of bed, making noise in the bathroom, bumping around, brushing his teeth and I lie in bed and I forget that anyone loves me and I'm too scared to call out to him. I lie there hoping he'll walk into our bedroom. And then he does.

EDDIE. *(To audience:)* I'm gonna get a dog.

BOB. *(To audience:)* My bed has white sheets, a white duvet, a yellow blanket, a pink blanket, a green blanket, and a pink brown and green mohair blanket, and two pillows. The yellow blanket is hidden, I don't like it, it's ugly. The pink blanket is hidden, I don't like it, it has holes. The green blanket is Dutch. The mohair blanket sits on top. It was my grandmother's and it reminds me of her long marble hallway, it's careful and it's clean and it's cool. And I have two pillows, because I am hopeful.

(MARNIE enters.)

MARNIE. You have a pen?

FRANK. Yeah I think somewhere.

MARNIE. I have to make a list of people I got to tell.

(MARNIE and FRANK sit in a pew, making her list.)

FRANK. Ok, who?

MARNIE. My Mom and Dad.

My brother.

My grandma. My grandpa. My nana.

My cousin Martha. My cousin Lisa. My other cousin
Lisa. All my cousins. All my. My aunts. My uncles.

I can't.

FRANK. You can.

MARNIE. My parents' friends. The Nashes. The Petits. The
Howards.

FRANK. Your parents can tell them.

MARNIE. My parents' neighbors.

FRANK. Your Mom and Dad can tell them too.

MARNIE. My friends.

I can't Frank.

FRANK. Marnie. You can.

MARNIE. Gary's parents.

Gary.

I can't.

FRANK. Ok.

Ok.

MARNIE. I can't. I can't.

I made too big a mistake.

(They sit in a pew.

Back with the others:

MELISSA *enters.)*

BOB. Did you see them?

MELISSA. Nope.

EDDIE. Let's go home.

MELISSA. We're not going home. Bob. Linda. We're not going home.

BOB. We made a promise.

EDDIE. (*To Bob:*) We're not going to be able to help them. She's all worked up. You don't think people can fall in love. I'm dizzy.

LINDA. I drink too much.

EDDIE. She drinks too much. What makes you think we can help our friends when we can't even?

BOB. (*Hisses:*) I think people can fall in love.

EDDIE. Yeah. Sure.

MELISSA. We're not leaving here until we stop Marnie from kissing that guy. We made a promise. Sit down.

(They all do.

MELISSA *stares into the distance. Then:*

The world tilts, **MELISSA,** **LINDA,** **BOB** *and* **EDDIE** *slide offstage,* **MARNIE** *and* **FRANK** *slide onstage.*

The world tilts back the other way, **BOB** *slides back onstage.)*

BOB. Marnie!

(The world tilts, **BOB** *slides offstage.* **MARNIE** *and* **FRANK** *hold onto something and manage to stay onstage.*

The world tilts back, **BOB** *and* **EDDIE** *slide onstage.)*

BOB. Marnie!

EDDIE. Frankie!

(The world tilts, **BOB** *and* **EDDIE** *slide offstage.* **MARNIE** *and* **FRANK** *manage to stay onstage.*

The world tilts back, **BOB** *and* **EDDIE** *and* **LINDA** *slide onstage.)*

BOB. Marnie!

EDDIE. Frankie!

LINDA. Melissa!

(The world's stomach rumbles. Then: **MELISSA** *enters. They all eye each other.)*

MELISSA. Well.

MARNIE. Hi Melissa.

MELISSA. Marnie. Where the hell have you been?

MARNIE. I had to go off and think.

MELISSA. Yeah well we were worried sick. We don't even know that guy.

MARNIE. He's my banker.

MELISSA. That's right. He's a banker and you just went off with him. Just left us and ran off into the night, drunk and stupid and we had to go looking for you and you're with some banker and you're ridiculous and drunk and stupid.

LINDA. I'm drunk too.

MELISSA. Shut up Linda.

MARNIE. I'm not going to marry Gary.

(Lights get bright for a second. Everyone but **LINDA** *sobers up.)*

MELISSA. What?

BOB. Oh no here we go.

MELISSA. What?

MARNIE. I'm not.

LINDA. See! I told you! She's not going to marry Gary!

BOB. What are you talking about Marnie?

MARNIE. Bob I'm

MELISSA. Yes you are.

LINDA. Yes you are!

MARNIE. No I'm not.

LINDA. No she's not!

MELISSA. Yes you are Don't be stupid Of course you are

LINDA. You're being stupid!

MARNIE. I am not.

LINDA. This is terrible!

(Sits down. Cries.)

MELISSA. You're giving me a headache. Anyone got any ibuprophen? I gotta get a glass of water.

MARNIE. I changed my mind. A girl's got a right to change her mind. Linda.

MELISSA. No you don't!

MARNIE. It's ok Linda.

LINDA. It's not ok! We bought dresses! Bob!

BOB. They bought dresses.

EDDIE. Frank She's a bride

MELISSA. Yeah.

EDDIE. She's someone else's fiancee

MELISSA. Yeah!

LINDA. And we already bought our dresses!

FRANK. She doesn't want to marry him.

BOB. Oh no here we go.

FRANK. She doesn't.

MARNIE. I don't.

EDDIE. You don't?

MELISSA. She does too!

BOB. Talk some sense into him Eddie.

EDDIE. He's not going to listen to me.

BOB. Eddie.

EDDIE. He doesn't listen to anyone.

FRANK. I do too.

EDDIE. You didn't listen to Priscilla.

FRANK. Well maybe I've learned how to. You think about that Eddie?

EDDIE. Ok then Ok You gonna listen? She's drunk.

FRANK. Who?

EDDIE. Her!

FRANK. Eddie.

EDDIE. She is!

MELISSA. Yeah!

BOB. Yeah.

LINDA. Yeah!

MARNIE. I'm not drunk.

MELISSA. Yeah you are.

EDDIE. You are.

LINDA. Marnie.

FRANK. You are.

MARNIE. Only a little.

BOB. Well.

EDDIE. (*To* **FRANK.**) And you're drunk too.

LINDA. And I'm drunk.

FRANK. (*Ignores Linda.*) Yeah so?

EDDIE. You're both drunk. But she's gonna sober up.

BOB. She is.

FRANK. What do you know You never even try to fall in love.

LINDA. We bought dresses! And GLOVES!

EDDIE. When she's sober she's gonna wanna marry him.

BOB. She is.

MELISSA. You are!

MARNIE. I am not!

BOB. You wanted to before.

MELISSA. You love him.

FRANK. She's so pretty.

MARNIE. Oh Frankie.

(*They kiss. The city tilts. They all stumble.*)

MELISSA. God-frickin-damn Marnie Stop it!

MARNIE. What?

MELISSA. You love him. You love Gary. Listen to me.

MARNIE. I do. I know. I do.

FRANK. What?

MARNIE. I do.

EDDIE. See?

LINDA. See Frank see?

MELISSA. She loves him. She loves him.

EDDIE. She loves him. Frank. Listen to her.

FRANK. You do?

MARNIE. I do.

EDDIE. Listen to her What'd she just say?

FRANK. You do?

MARNIE. But.

FRANK. But what?

BOB. But what?

MELISSA. But what?

FRANK. Hey.

But what Marnie?

MARNIE. I'm not in love with him. I wanted to be but I'm not. I'm not Melissa. I'm not. I'm not. I'm sorry.

FRANK. See? She's not in love with him!

MELISSA. You made a promise. You made a promise! Are you just gonna break that promise?

MARNIE. Just because Jason treated you rotten doesn't mean I have to marry Gary.

LINDA. Marnie.

EDDIE. Marnie.

BOB. Marnie.

MARNIE. People change their minds!

BOB. Still.

LINDA. Jason.

MARNIE. They do!

LINDA. (*Mutters:*) You don't have to bring up Jason.

BOB. Yeah.

MARNIE. People make poor choices Make mistakes Get to change their minds.

MELISSA. No.

MARNIE. Yes.

MELISSA. No.

MARNIE. I'm dishonest and Gary is perfectly happy not hearing the truth from me. We're a terrible match.

MELISSA. You're a stupid selfish woman. You don't care about anyone.

FRANK. Melissa.

EDDIE. Frank, don't.

MARNIE. No?

MELISSA. No.

FRANK. Melissa.

EDDIE. Don't. Frank. Let'm.

MARNIE. All I do is care about people.

MELISSA. (*Clucks.*)

MARNIE. What they want. How I can make them happy. It's true. It's how I got into this mess.
And he doesn't love me.

MELISSA. He does.

MARNIE. He wants to be married.

MELISSA. Same thing!

MARNIE. No.

BOB. No.

LINDA. No.

MELISSA. Yes it is!

BOB. No. It isn't.

MELISSA. She took Gary He's a good guy He's a good guy and she strung him along She made him promises She tangled up his heart She made him hope Made him hope
And now he's under her heel and she's just
And his life is ruined

MARNIE. Shut up.

MELISSA. She's ruined his life. You ruined his life!

MARNIE. That's it. I'm done with you.

MELISSA. What?

MARNIE. That's it Melissa. That's it. Done.

MELISSA. What?

MARNIE. I'm not listening to you I'm finished. Linda, make her leave.

LINDA. What Marnie?

MARNIE. Bob get her out of here.

BOB. Marnie.

MELISSA. Marnie.

MARNIE. I'M NOT TALKING TO YOU ANYMORE!

MELISSA. You coming Linda?

LINDA. What?

MARNIE. Linda.

LINDA. What?

MELISSA. Linda?

LINDA. Marnie You're the reason the world is scary I can't People changing their minds What if Jack Jason left Melissa You're leaving Gary What if Jack This is terrible!

MELISSA. She doesn't want me here any more. Are you coming?

LINDA. Come on Marnie Melissa come on Don't

MELISSA. She's finished with me.

LINDA. Marnie We've all been friends forever

MARNIE. No.

LINDA. Marnie come on

MARNIE. Go with her It's ok I'll call you later

LINDA. Bob

BOB. Go on.

LINDA. (*Quietly:*) Marnie. Please.

(*Then:* **LINDA** *and* **MELISSA** *exit.*)

MARNIE. Because even if he's in love with me and, I can do that, I can be the person someone is in love with, I can do that Bob, I can, what I can't do, I'm not so good at being the person in love with someone else. So

BOB. It's hard to be alone Marnie.

MARNIE. Bobby?

BOB. Are you sure you want to be alone?

MARNIE. I can't marry him.

BOB. Ok.

MARNIE. I can't.

BOB. Marnie

MARNIE. What do you know about love?

BOB. Ok.

(*BOB exits.*)

MARNIE. That was. I just

(*Long long difficult pause.*)

I'm going to go grab that cab.

(**MARNIE** *exits. They watch her leave.*)

EDDIE. Huh.

FRANK. Come on Eddie. I gotta go home and clean my car.

THREE.

LINDA. (*In a spotlight. Sings.*)
I saw the city
I saw the city
The city opened its mouth
I saw its teeth
I saw the city
I saw the dragon
And it turned
The world turned
Walking on the path
It follows
Walking on the path
It follows me

Something is wrong
Something is wrong inside
Something is wrong
Something is wrong inside
And I was home
I brought the dragon home
I brought the city home
And Its teeth

It's at the end of the hall
At the end of the hall
AND IF THE DOOR OPENS
IF I SEE IT
AND I
AND

FOUR.

(The hangover.

It is the next day. Early afternoon.

The street near **BOB**'s *bakery.* **MARNIE** *sits on the sidewalk curb.* **BOB**, *wearing a baker's apron, enters.)*

MARNIE. Hi.

BOB. Hi. What are you doing sitting out here?

MARNIE. *(Looks at him.)*

BOB. You look tired.

MARNIE. I am. I had such a headache when I woke up this morning. I took four Tylenols.

BOB. I bet.

MARNIE. I called Linda

(Pause.)

BOB. How's she doing?

MARNIE. She's Ok. She said she woke up and she opened her eyes and it was so sunny and she got up and went out into her garden and you know how her tomato plants are doing so well and her zucchini and her eggplant and she was all happy and picked some She said they were such bright red tomatoes and she was all "I'm going to make ratatouille!" and she was cutting up the vegetables and all of sudden she said she had this terrible thought She thought "I don't remember anyone else talking last night." And she was so panicked.

BOB. She's gotta stop drinking.

MARNIE. Well.

BOB. Did you talk?

MARNIE. Yeah. Linda and I We're always gonna be ok. She made me laugh. She read me something this guy Thoreau said. I didn't understand it.

(Melissa enters. She and Marnie look at each other. Melissa exits.)

BOB. You gonna talk to her?

MARNIE. Bob.

BOB. Are you?

MARNIE. No.

(Long pause.)

I talked to him.

BOB. Gary?

MARNIE. This morning.

BOB. Huh.

MARNIE. Yeah. He's really upset. He doesn't believe me but I can kinda tell he does.

BOB. You give him back his ring?

MARNIE. Uh hm. He wanted me to keep it but I gave it back to him. That's what made him cry.

(Pause.)

I kept smiling at him but.

And I told my Mom and Dad. And my Mom cried and then she was really mad. And went and made the beds.

My Dad just

BOB. They'll

MARNIE. *(Cries.)* I'm sorry I said that about you. Last night. It was mean.

BOB. It's ok.

MARNIE. I am Bobby I'm sorry. You know lots about love.

BOB. It's ok. I really don't. You were right. Why do you think I hang around you guys? I gotta learn about this stupid love stuff somewhere. I figure one of you guys is gonna figure it out.

MARNIE. Maybe Can I Um

Can I tell you something?

BOB. Is it going to hurt my feelings?

MARNIE. No.

BOB. Is it?

MARNIE. No it's just
  Something I noticed?

BOB. Ok.

MARNIE. Can I?

BOB. Yeah yeah Tell Me.

MARNIE. Well I was wondering
  Do you think maybe you love too hard?

BOB. What?

MARNIE. Maybe you could love a little easier. Is all.

  (Pause.)

BOB. That's what he said.

MARNIE. Yeah.

BOB. That's what he said.

MARNIE. Well maybe. Maybe he was trying to tell you
  something.

BOB. So
  How?

MARNIE. Maybe
  When you get nervous Or something isn't
  You could take a breath.
  Instead of doing anything.

BOB. Really?

MARNIE. Maybe?

BOB. That'd be a big change for me.

MARNIE. If it's something you gotta do, you gotta do it.
  Right?

BOB. I don't think I could.

MARNIE. You could do it.

BOB. You think?

MARNIE. I don't know how I'm supposed to do what I've
  got to do.

BOB. You'll figure it out.

MARNIE. "You think?"

BOB. I know It's really hard not being who people want you to be. If there's anything I know, it's that. Remember when my Mom She was all "No son of mine" "My son isn't going to" Remember how upset she was about me? She didn't want me to be a baker.

But. She's ok with it now.

Honesty's hard It's

That's why people are always saying you gotta

It's a simple thing but it's the hardest thing.

But you gotta.

MARNIE. You done?

BOB. Your problem is Something shows up and you should say something and you're "I gotta get out of here."

MARNIE. You done Bob?

LINDA. (*Enters.*) Hi. Hey Bob.

MARNIE. Hi.

BOB. Hi Linda.

LINDA. Hi Bob.

> (*Pause.*)

> Last night huh? It was.

BOB. Yeah.

LINDA. Huh?

BOB. Yeah.

> (*Pause.*)

LINDA. Crazy.

> (*Laughs.*)

> I loved it when

> (*Pause.*)

> It was.

MARNIE. Hm.

> (*Long awkward pause.*)

LINDA. (*Off-handed.*) Jack and I are going to stop drinking. Yeah. He doesn't want to drink any more. Because he. I talked to him. So I'm going to With him.

MARNIE. Oh.

BOB. Yeah?

LINDA. He doesn't want to any more. Because he.

(*Long pause.*)

I don't really want to drink any more either.

MARNIE. That sounds. Actually.

BOB. Yeah.

LINDA. (*A short laugh.*

Then:)

Did you tell him?

MARNIE. No.

BOB. Tell me what?

LINDA. Why not?

MARNIE. I was just about to.

LINDA. You should just tell him.

MARNIE. I'm gonna.

LINDA. Oh.

BOB. Tell me what?

MARNIE. I came to tell you I'm not going to work at the bakery any more.

BOB. What?

MARNIE. I'm going to get an apartment in the city.

BOB. Oh. Why?

LINDA. Because she's gotta.

MARNIE. Linda.

LINDA. Sorry.

BOB. Why?

MARNIE. Because I have to.

(*They sit in silence. Then:*

FRANK *and* **EDDIE** *enter.*)

BOB. So when are you

FRANK. Hi Marnie.

MARNIE. Hi.

FRANK. Hi. Hi. Awesome. I hoped I'd

EDDIE. Hi Bob. Hi Linda.

BOB. Hey Eddie.

LINDA. Hi.

BOB. You found us.

EDDIE. Yeah. The Sunshine Bakery.

LINDA. Hi Frank.

EDDIE. (*Sits.*) I'm being moral support.

BOB. Oh huh.

LINDA. For what?

FRANK. Hi Bob.

BOB. Frank.

FRANK. Um Marnie?

MARNIE. Yeah?

FRANK. Can I talk to you for a minute?

MARNIE. Sure What?

FRANK. Over here?

(**BOB, EDDIE** *and* **LINDA** *sit on the curb and watch.*)

BOB. Oh no here we go.

MARNIE. Why?

FRANK. Please?

MARNIE. Ok.

FRANK. You still not marrying Gary?

MARNIE. No.

FRANK. You're sure?

MARNIE. Yeah.

FRANK. Because, if you're not marrying him, can I take you out to dinner?

MARNIE. What?

FRANK. I want to take you out to dinner tonight.

MARNIE. I heard you.

FRANK. Since you're not marrying him.

MARNIE. Frank Don't start with me. Did you just hear what he asked me?

FRANK. I do.

MARNIE. I'm warning you. Listen to me

FRANK. What? I just want to take you out to dinner -

MARNIE. Goddamn it!

(*Storms out.* **EDDIE, BOB** *and* **LINDA** *sit watching.*

Pause.

Storms in.)

Frank You He's You You're a pain in the ass!

BOB. Ok then!

LINDA. Ok!

FRANK. I just wanted

MARNIE. You're a huge frigging pain in the ass!

FRANK. (*Shouts.*) I just want to take you to dinner!

MARNIE. (*Shouts.*) Yeah well! You're a huge frigging pain!

FRANK. Yeah!

MARNIE. I gotta move out of our apartment, I gotta start over, and you!

FRANK. Ok.

MARNIE. I've gotta spend some time

FRANK. Hey watch this.

(**FRANK** *dances. Should be a simple solo love dance. Not too short. Sincere and a bit funny. He means it.*)

MARNIE. Frank.

FRANK. I couldn't sleep last night. So I made you that. Cause I was thinking after you left and all night – I could love you like that Marnie – the way you want.

MARNIE. (*Quiet.*) Oh you could Frank?

FRANK. I could.

MARNIE. What way is that?

FRANK. Me being in love, but not too much, and letting you be yourself.

MARNIE. Frank.

FRANK. (FRANK *dances a little.*)

MARNIE. Frank.

FRANK. I was listening to you.

MARNIE. Frank.

FRANK. (*Smiles.*)

MARNIE. Don't smile at me that way.

FRANK. Yeah. Ok. No.

> (*Smiles.*)

MARNIE. I never learned to fall in love. I don't know how to do it.

FRANK. You could learn with me.

MARNIE. I don't think so. Listen to me Frank. I'm telling you the truth: Don't smile at me.

FRANK. Marnie.

> (**MARNIE** *doesn't answer him.*)
>
> Ok. Eddie You coming?

EDDIE. I'm going to hang out here for a bit.

FRANK. You are?

EDDIE. I'll hook a ride home.

FRANK. Oh. Ok. Ok. See ya.

BOB. See ya Frank.

> (**FRANK** *exits. Pause. Then:*)

LINDA. You ok?

BOB. Sure she's ok. That was good You see her? She just told him That was good.

LINDA. Yeah.

MARNIE. (*Deep, frightened breath.*)

BOB. Now go in there and tell Melissa Tell her what you

MARNIE. No.

BOB. Come on champ.

MARNIE. No.

BOB. Marnie

MARNIE. No. Bob. I'm not going to. She and me, we're.

   (Pause.)

LINDA. Ok.

MARNIE. I'm not going to.

LINDA. Ok.

   (Pause.)

BOB. Ok.

LINDA. Let's go over to my house.

BOB. Yeah Linda take her over to your house.

LINDA. Ok.

BOB. That's what you should do.

LINDA. Ok Bob ok.

BOB. What?

LINDA. What.

MARNIE. Ok.

BOB. Ok.

LINDA. Ok.

MARNIE. Ok. See ya Eddie.

EDDIE. Bye.

LINDA. Ok. Bye.

BOB. Bye. See ya Marnie.

MARNIE. Bye Bobby.

   *(**MARNIE** and **LINDA** exit.)*

BOB. Kids. Jeez.

EDDIE. I know huh.

BOB. You gotta tell them how to do everything.

EDDIE. Right?

BOB. I thought that dance was going to work.

EDDIE. He's probably going to call her tomorrow. Knowing Frankie.

BOB. Tell him not to.

EDDIE. He's brave isn't he? He just goes for it He It's brave to put all your cards out on the table like that.

(Pause.)

BOB. Oh hey I wanted to. I have your ring.

EDDIE. Oh. I forgot we. Yeah. You can keep mine if you want. I like yours.

BOB. Oh. Ok. Well.

EDDIE. Unless you want it back. No. Here.

BOB. No no you can keep it.

EDDIE. Really?

BOB. Sure.

EDDIE. Oh right on. Cause I like yours.

BOB. I like this one.

EDDIE. Cool.

BOB. This one's good.

EDDIE. Ok then.

BOB. Ok then.

EDDIE. Hey I wanted to show you Remember how I wouldn't

*(Still sitting on the curb **EDDIE** does a very small tap step.)*

BOB. That's.

EDDIE. I didn't mean to be rude last night.

BOB. No.

EDDIE. I get shy. I don't know why.

BOB. How do you do that?

EDDIE. It's easy.

BOB. Yeah right it's easy. It looks hard.

EDDIE. No it is. Watch.

*(Still sitting **EDDIE** shows **BOB** a very very simple tap step.)*

Try it. First. Yeah. Then. Yeah ok. No. Yeah. Right. Right?

*(**EDDIE** kisses **BOB** quickly.)*

BOB. Got tired of waiting huh?

EDDIE. You gonna make this hard on me?

BOB. No. No.

EDDIE. (*Looks at* **BOB.**)

    (*Pause.*)

BOB. (*Takes breath.*) No.

EDDIE. Ok then.

BOB. Ok then.

EDDIE. Ok.

    (*They sit.*)

END.

Also by
Adam Bock...

The Receptionist

The Thugs

Please visit our website **samuelfrench.com** for complete
descriptions and licensing information

CPSIA information can be obtained at www.ICGtesting.com
Printed in the USA
LVOW070937070713

341704LV00003B/167/P